Paul looked into YOUNG ADULTS
his parents' bedroom
and saw Tiffany.

She was reading his mother's diary. Paul's face felt hot. "You aren't supposed to do that," he said. "That's private."

Tiffany put the diary down. "Spies do this stuff all the time. You don't know much about being a spy, do you?" She jumped up from the bed and pulled open his mother's dresser drawer.

"Stop that," Paul said loudly.

"I'm not doing anything. I'm just looking. People hide things in their drawers, you know. . . . Hey," said Tiffany. "Look at this. Cigarettes."

Cigarettes! But his Mom didn't smoke. Or did she? Tiffany was stirring up *real* trouble!

Tiffany, the Disaster

Janice Harrell

A MINSTREL® BOOK

PUBLISHED BY POCKET BOOKS

New York   London   Toronto   Sydney   Tokyo   Singapore

A MINSTREL PAPERBACK *ORIGINAL*

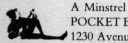

A Minstrel Book published by
POCKET BOOKS, a division of Simon & Schuster Inc.
1230 Avenue of the Americas, New York, NY 10020

ISBN: 0-671-72860-1

First Minstrel Books printing November 1992

10 9 8 7 6 5 4 3 2 1

A MINSTREL BOOK and colophon are registered trademarks
of Simon & Schuster Inc.

Cover art by Lina Levy

Printed in the U.S.A.

Tiffany, the Disaster

Chapter
One

Paul was playing at being a shark. He swam with one hand held out of the water like a fin. It was easy for him because he was a good swimmer. He could go in the deep end if he wanted, but he liked the shallow end. That was where the action was. He stopped for a minute and shook water off his hair. "I'm a great white shark," he said loudly. "That's the kind that can swallow you in one gulp." He put his head back under water and kicked off. He swam very fast. Myra Hux had to jump out of his way. She hit her head on the pool ladder and started to cry. The lifeguard's whistle shrieked in Paul's ear.

"Okay. That's enough," said the lifeguard, looking down at Paul. "Out of the pool. Stay out until I say you can go back in. Understand?"

Paul climbed out and shook the water out of his ears. He blinked the blurry chlorine out of his eyes and looked around curiously. Something was wrong. Why wasn't his father yelling at him?

That was when he spotted the girl standing by his father's deck chair. She had blue eyes, short, straight blond hair, and sturdy legs. Instead of a bathing suit, she had on shorts and a T-shirt.

"Why do you wear that funny hat?" she asked his father.

"To keep my head from getting sunburned." Mr. Fenner smiled at her. "I don't have as much hair on mine as you have on yours."

"Can I try it on?" asked the girl. Mr. Fenner handed it to her.

Paul figured his father should be paying attention to him and not the girl. "The lifeguard made me get out of the pool," he said. "But it wasn't my fault. Myra yelled so he thought I was killing her, but I never touched her."

"I'll bet," said his father, glancing over at

2

him. Mr. Fenner took his hat back and put it on his head. It did look funny. It was a floppy cotton hat that could be put in the washing machine when it got dirty. "You and Tiffany here are almost the same age," he told Paul. "She's going into second grade and you're going into third. Maybe you'll even be in the same car pool. Tiffany tells me her family is moving into the Palmers' old house."

Oh, no, Paul thought. This girl was going to live almost next door! She was half a foot taller than he was, too. It was settled, he thought gloomily. He was going to be a midget. Life as a midget was pretty tough to face when it was ninety degrees outside and the lifeguard wouldn't let you back in the pool.

Paul looked at Tiffany suspiciously. He thought it was funny the way she had started talking to his father. Most of the kids Paul knew hardly spoke to his parents, even if they had been coming over to Paul's house their whole lives practically. Tiffany wasn't just talking, either, she was trying on his dad's hat. How pushy could you get?

"Your hat smells funny," said Tiffany. "Do

4

you put something on your hair that makes it smell that way?"

Mr. Fenner looked uncomfortable. "Just a little something to keep it in place on top," he said. He didn't like people to know that he used hair spray where his hair was thin.

Tiffany turned to Paul. "I'm going to take swimming lessons. I'm going to learn to swim fast."

"You don't know how to swim?" Paul exclaimed. "Gah! How old are you anyway?"

"Quite a few people don't learn to swim until they're grown up, Paul," said Mr. Fenner.

"I could swim the pool length when I was— How old was I, Dad?"

"Five."

"Yeah. I even get to go off the high dive if I want."

"I'll probably do that, too," said Tiffany. "But now my mother is going to take me shopping and buy me a lot of new clothes."

"Tiffany!" A tall blond woman in a tennis dress bore down on them. "I thought you were right behind me, and when I turned around you were gone."

"I wanted to look at the swimming pool," Tiffany said. Paul felt as if she were measuring her height against his. She was a whole lot taller.

"I was signing Tiffany up for swimming lessons," the woman said to Mr. Fenner. "We're leaving tomorrow for a family reunion to introduce Tiff to all the folks, and I wanted to sign her up before we go."

Paul felt confused. He could have sworn the blond woman was Jeff Davis's mom. Jeff Davis was older than Paul. Paul didn't know him too well, but he knew Jeff didn't have a little sister named Tiffany.

Paul sneaked a look back at the pool. Myra and Suzy Hart were taking turns diving for shiny pennies. Paul wondered if the lifeguard was keeping an eye on him still. Maybe he would try sticking just one foot in the water.

Tiffany and her mother went off in the direction of the tennis courts, and after a minute, Paul forgot about them. He sat on the edge of the pool and dangled his feet in the water.

"I thought the lifeguard told you to stay out of the pool," said his dad.

"That was a long time ago. Anyway, I'm

not in the pool. Only my feet are in." Paul could feel the sun hot on his shoulders. He kicked his feet until the water churned. Paul was itching to get in. He hated to sit on the edge when the water was where everything was happening. It was so crowded that kids kept bumping into one another even when they weren't trying to.

After a minute Paul leaned back on his elbows and lowered himself into the water up to his swimsuit. He was almost completely in, but not really. If the lifeguard yelled at him, he could still say he was sitting on the side of the pool. His elbows were resting on the edge.

Paul's mother had made him wear a Day-glo orange swimsuit. She worried that the lifeguard would not notice him. Paul worried about just the opposite. He wanted the lifeguard to leave him alone. If he kept inching down the way he was going, soon the Day-glo swimsuit would be completely under water. Maybe the lifeguard wouldn't see it. He felt the cold water against his skin and he shivered.

Suddenly the lifeguard's whistle shrieked. Paul's stomach turned over. He jumped out of the pool.

"Break!" yelled the lifeguard. "Time for break. Everybody out."

Paul scrambled to his feet. The cement was almost too hot to stand on except right beside the pool where water had splashed. He was glad the lifeguard had not been yelling at him. For a second he had been worried about that. He went over to his father's deck chair. "Talk about rotten luck," he said. "Now they're having a break! That lifeguard is supposed to take a ten-minute break but half the time he takes fifteen. I'll bet I've already been out ten already. It's not fair."

"Life's not fair," said Paul's dad. He closed his thick book. Mr. Fenner planned to read all six volumes of *The History of the English-Speaking Peoples* over the summer. He said that with all the time he put in keeping an eye on Paul at the pool, that should be a cinch. He was a teacher at the local college, and he had a lot of time off in the summer. "It's time for us to go home anyway."

For once Paul did not beg to stay longer. If he wasn't going to get to go in the pool, he might as well go home. Besides, he was getting hungry.

Chapter
Two

Sometimes when Paul and his father got home late from the pool, Paul's mother had dinner ready. Or if she had a hard day at work they would send out for pizza. Paul's mother was a social worker and she had a lot of hard days at work. Paul was hoping this was going to be a pizza night. He liked his mother to have a good day, but he really liked pizza, too.

"That girl Tiffany is weird," Paul said. "Why did she want to try on your hat? And that lady who was acting like her mother was really Jeff Davis's mother. Jeff Davis doesn't have any little sister named Tiffany. You can take it from me he doesn't. You know, now that I think of it, there was a movie kind of like that on television. This girl had been kidnapped, you see, and—"

"Jeff Davis has a little sister named Tiffany now, sport. The Davises are adopting Tiffany. Your mother told me all about it."

Paul's mouth fell open. "You mean they're just now getting around to adopting her and she's going to be in the second grade? That's totally weird."

"Don't keep saying *weird* over and over again, Paul. I'm a patient man, but it's beginning to get to me. Think, analyze, and describe what you see, okay?"

"I did," said Paul, surprised. "That's how I figured out that she was weird."

His father sighed. "I give up. What I was trying to say was the Davises decided to adopt an older child since Mrs. Davis teaches school and wouldn't be home all day. They thought a child closer in age to Jeff would be better, too. That way the two kids could be company for each other."

Paul knew all about adoption. He was adopted himself. For years his mother had read him a book about how great it was to be chosen. Finally he had told her that he pre-

10

ferred books about quicksand, lightning, tarantulas, or snakes. He liked to be prepared for every possible disaster.

"What was wrong with this Tiffany?" he asked. "Why didn't she get chosen when she was a baby?"

"Maybe she wasn't available for adoption until she was older. That happens sometimes."

Already Paul had a feeling that Tiffany was going to be one of the disasters he prepared for. He didn't like the sound of any of this. Paul's parents were really into this adoption stuff. They even had a special supper club. Everybody in the supper club had adopted a kid. Every month they had dinner at somebody else's house. While the grown-ups ate by candlelight in the dining room, the kids ate hamburgers in the kitchen.

Paul liked that because the kids who came were his friends Suzy Hart and Billy Blakely. Paul liked them. What if his parents asked the Davises to join? If Tiffany's parents started coming to the supper club he would have to play with her.

When they got home Paul remembered

something. His parents' dinner table would hold only six. He had heard his mom say lots of times that even six people made it crowded. He poked his head into the dining room, checked out the table and smiled. Six chairs. Six placemats. No room for Tiffany's folks. When he went into the kitchen to eat his share of the pizza, he was humming a tune.

Chapter
Three

When school started, Paul was in a car pool with four girls. That was bad. What was even worse was that one of the girls was Tiffany.

On the first day of school Suzy Hart's mother drove. When she came to pick the children up at the end of the day, the back of her station wagon was filled with paper bags. She had just come from shopping. All the children got in and Mrs. Hart drove away from the school. Tiffany turned around in her seat and started peeking in the paper bags.

"Is someone out of her seat belt?" said Mrs. Hart. She looked in the rearview mirror. "I'm going to have to stop the car if everybody doesn't get buckled in by the time I count to three." Mrs. Hart counted slowly. "One—two—three."

Tiffany pulled a stack of plastic flowerpots out of a bag. "What are these for?" she asked.

Paul stared out the window. He tried to look as if he had nothing to do with the girls in the car. He was only along for the ride.

Mrs. Hart pulled the car over to the side and parked. She was a nervous driver. "Tiffany, you have to sit down and buckle your seat belt. What are you doing?"

Tiffany sat down and buckled her seat belt. "Just looking in the bags."

"Nothing very interesting in the bags."

"I was just looking," said Tiffany.

"Mama, we're going to be late for my piano lesson," said Suzy.

"We're going, Suzy. Now that everybody is buckled in."

Suzy sighed. Paul knew what she was thinking. Tiffany was a pain. He could have told Suzy that.

That afternoon when Mrs. Fenner came in from work she was carrying two card tables.

"I borrowed these from the Harts," she said. She leaned the card tables against the couch. "How was school, sweetheart?"

"Okay."

"How do you like your new teacher?"

"Okay."

"Are any of your friends in your class?"

"Some."

"You don't want to talk about it or what?"

"I said it was okay, didn't I? What are the card tables for?"

"The supper club is coming over Saturday night, and our dining room table just isn't big enough. I'm going to put card tables in the living room instead." She looked around. "With little dishes of flowers and white table-cloths on each one, they'll look fine."

Paul was suspicious. "Our table was always big enough before."

"That was before we asked the Davises. You know, our new neighbors?"

Oh, no. Tiffany was going to be coming to dinner after all. I knew it, thought Paul.

"Why do we have to have them?"

"Goodness, why do you care who we have to dinner?"

15

"I guess they're going to bring Tiffany."

"You don't even know her, Paul. Don't be such a pickle. When the kids get here, you always have a good time. I wonder if I should have borrowed a tablecloth," said Mrs. Fenner. She went into the hall to check in the linen closet.

It was hopeless, Paul realized. There was no way out. If he fell into quicksand, he could just float on his back. Or if he was in an open field and smelled ozone and felt his hair stand on end so he knew lightning was about to strike, he could throw himself on the ground with only his fingers and toes touching. He'd probably survive the lightning. Paul knew a lot of neat ways to save himself from danger, but he didn't know any way to protect himself from girls named Tiffany.

Saturday morning was ruined because Paul couldn't stop thinking about how Tiffany was coming to dinner. He didn't even enjoy his favorite cartoon, *Captain Power and the Soldiers of the Future*. Over the sound of the cartoons, he heard the roar of the vacuum cleaner in the living room. His parents always spent the day cleaning before the supper club came.

16

The phone rang. Paul's parents couldn't hear it because of the vacuum cleaner so Paul went into their bedroom and picked up the phone.

"Hello?"

"Paul? This is Granny. I'm home!"

Paul's grandmother had been on a trip to England and Scotland.

"Did you have a good time, Granny?"

"I sure did. Even if it rained every day, it was wonderful fun. I'll be glad to see my Pauley again, though."

"Did you bring me anything?" Paul was proud that he had remembered to ask if she had a good time before he asked about his present.

She laughed. "I sure did, pumpkin."

Paul's heart began to pound. He had told his grandmother before she left that what he really wanted was a *skean dhu,* a kind of dagger he could fit into his sock. Paul was sure his mother would let him have it because he couldn't cut himself with it. It wasn't sharp on the sides. Just pointy at the top. They were only used to stab an enemy in the heart. A *skean dhu* would be handy to have if there was

17

ever a massacre like they had in Scotland in the old days. Paul's book *Weapons Through the Ages* had a color picture of one with diamonds and rubies on the handle.

Paul's mother had told him to talk to his grandmother about other things besides presents. He didn't say anything about the dagger. "Did you happen to see any ghosts?" he asked.

"Well, I did stay at an inn that was four hundred years old. The owners said it had a ghost."

"A boy ghost or a girl ghost?"

"A lady ghost. She was supposed to go around in her nightie wailing for her lost love. None of us on the tour happened to catch her the particular night we were there."

When it came to ghosts, Paul preferred soldier ghosts with chains or sailor ghosts with seaweed. A wail wasn't bad. A wail in the middle of the night could be pretty creepy. He was sorry his grandmother had not heard it. "Do you want to talk to Mom? She's cleaning up. The supper club is coming over tonight."

"No. Don't bother her then. She won't

have time to talk now. I'll come over tomorrow morning."

"Uh, Granny? Don't forget anything when
you come over, okay?"

Paul's grandmother laughed.

Chapter Four

When the supper club came that night, Paul was feeling happy. He was thinking of his *skean dhu.* Even having Tiffany in the house could not spoil his evening. The four kids ate hamburgers at the kitchen table. Paul put a lot of ketchup on his. He had explained to his mother that he didn't need to eat broccoli because ketchup was full of vitamins.

"I'm in the first reading group," boasted Tiffany.

Mrs. Fenner stuck her head in the kitchen door. "Everything okay in here? Do you have everything you need? Do you want more milk, Billy?"

Billy did not want more milk. His appetite had been spoiled by hearing that Tiffany was in the first reading group. Billy had to go to extra lessons all summer to help him with his reading. He was tired of hearing about reading. He especially didn't want to hear about people who were in the first reading group.

Paul did not like hearing about the first reading group either. He was in the second reading group. He wondered if the people at the adoption agency had gotten Tiffany's age wrong. Maybe she was really an eight-year-old kid disguised as a seven-year-old kid. That would explain why she was so tall and also why she was so good at reading.

"I want some more," said Tiffany.

Mrs. Fenner poured out more milk for Tiffany. Then she went back to the dining room.

Suzy said, "I brought a cassette tonight if anybody wants to watch it after we eat. *Ghostbusters II.*"

"I saw it three times," said Billy.

"I saw it, too," said Paul.

"We could play Life," said Suzy.

Tiffany gulped her milk down. "We could play spy," she said.

21

"Is that a game?" asked Billy.

"Yup. All we need are pencils and paper."

Paul did not trust her. "What do we do in this game?"

"We sneak around and listen to what people are saying and we write it down. I know a good place to hide," she said. "I'm going to hide behind that big chair in the living room."

"My mom doesn't like us to go in there when they're eating."

"You can't be a spy if you don't spy on people, can you?" said Tiffany. "That's the way you do it. Only we need pencil and paper. You have to write everything down in your spy notebook."

"No!" said Paul. He surprised himself. He did not usually say *no* so loudly. Tiffany just made him feel like shouting.

Tiffany shrugged. "We can do some other things." Paul was certain she did not mean they could play Life.

Tiffany got out of her chair, pushed open the kitchen door, and went off toward the bedrooms.

Paul and Suzy and Billy looked at one another. They did not know what to do.

"We better go with her," Suzy whispered. "She might do something."

Paul wondered what Suzy thought Tiffany might do. He was afraid to ask.

The three children went down the hall and began peeking into the bedrooms looking for Tiffany. Paul could hear the adults talking in the living room. He was sure they were talking about income tax or football or the P.T.A. Sometimes Paul listened to his parents' friends talking. They talked about those three things a lot. He thought it would be pretty boring to write that all down in a notebook.

Paul looked into his parents' bedroom and saw Tiffany. She was reading his mother's diary. Paul's face felt hot. "You aren't supposed to do that," he said. "That's private."

Tiffany put the diary down. "Spies do this stuff all the time. You don't know much about being a spy, do you?" She jumped up from the bed and pulled open his mother's dresser drawer.

"Stop that," Paul said loudly.

"I'm not doing anything. I'm just looking. People hide things in their drawers, you know. I wouldn't hide anything there. Too obvious. I would put it under the carpet or in the freezer."

"You're crazy."

"Hey," said Tiffany. "Look at this. Cigarettes."

"Let me see." Paul pushed Tiffany aside and stared at the carton of cigarettes in his mother's underwear drawer. "My mom doesn't smoke."

"That's what you think."

Paul frowned at Tiffany. She closed the drawer and opened the jewelry box on his mother's dresser.

"Get out of that." He pushed her hand away. A perfume bottle fell over. "Look what you made me do." Paul was glad the bottle didn't break. "You get out of here," he said, "or I'm going to go tell my mom."

Tiffany's blue eyes stared into his. "I don't care," she said. She did turn and walk out of the room. Paul could breathe better when she left. He straightened up the bottle of perfume. He made sure all the drawers were closed and that the diary was back in its place. Even though he put everything back, nothing seemed the same now that he knew about the cigarettes in his mother's drawer. Cigarettes had to mean that she smoked. She had told him herself how bad smoking was for you!

Chapter
Five

Y ou act like I'm dealing drugs," said Paul's mother the next morning.

"You told me it was bad for people to smoke," Paul repeated. "You told me I should never start smoking."

"She was right about that!" said Paul's father. He was reading the Sunday paper, but he had looked up when Paul and his mother started arguing.

"You hid those cigarettes in your drawer," Paul said, accusing her.

"Only because I didn't want to be a bad influence on you. I've tried everything to stop smoking. Nicotine chewing gum, even. I sent away for the Cancer Society's ten-step pro-

gram and I did every step except the last one—
stop. I don't smoke very much."

"What were you doing in your mother's
dresser drawers, anyway?" asked his father.
"We don't search through your private
things."

"It wasn't me. It was Tiffany. She's always
poking around in things. She was even reading your diary. I had to make her get out of
your room."

Mr. and Mrs. Fenner glanced at each other.

"Well, I told you she was weird, didn't I?"

"You did the right thing to make her leave
our room," said Mrs. Fenner. "I guess she's
having a little trouble settling down. We'll
have to be patient with her. I'm going to keep
trying to stop smoking, Paul. I promise."

"You ought to throw those cigarettes
away," said Paul. "I could throw them away
for you."

"No. But I will do my best to cut down,"
his mother said.

The doorbell rang. It was Paul's grandmother. She was wearing a flowered sundress.
She had put something on her gray hair to
make it blue.

28

"You're back!" Paul's mother hugged her. "How was it? Tell us everything."

"A ten-hour delay at Gatwick and a two-hour delay in New York! Am I glad to be home! Where's my Pauley?" Paul's grandmother held out her arms to him.

This time Paul could not stop himself. "Where's my present?" he said breathlessly.

"Paul!" said his mother.

"Now, Emmy, leave him alone. I've got it right here. It's hard to wait for surprises, isn't it?" Paul's grandmother reached into the shopping bag at her feet and took out a present wrapped in green paper.

It was large, flat, and square, the shape of a book.

Paul ripped the paper off.

It *was* a book. *Angus, Boy of Scotland*. Paul felt sick. "I guess you couldn't find a dagger, huh?" he said softly.

"I didn't think you'd have much use for a dagger in Meadowbrook Heights. Don't you like the book?"

"What do you say to Granny, Paul?" said Mrs. Fenner.

"Thank you," said Paul.

29

"Did you have a lot of rain?" asked Mr. Fenner. "Ben Jolley said it rained every day when he was over there."

"It never stopped raining. I suppose that's why they have all those lovely roses. It's a wonder I didn't come home with mildew behind my ears."

Paul's parents and his grandmother went into the kitchen. Paul stayed in the foyer staring at his present.

The front door flew open. Billy was hanging on to the doorknob. His bicycle was lying on top of the petunias planted along the front walk. "I saw your grandmother," he said. "Did she give you the dagger yet? Can I see it? Can I touch it?"

Paul held out the book. Billy's face fell. "That's it? That's the present?"

Paul was afraid if he said something he might cry. He felt hollow inside.

"I have an aunt who gives me things like that," said Billy. "For my birthday she gave me *What You Want to Know About Your Sewer System*. I don't want to know *anything* about my sewer system."

Paul saw Tiffany going by on the sidewalk

outside. She was riding on a scooter, pushing herself with one foot. All her clothes looked brand-new. "Shut the door," said Paul. "I don't want to look at that girl. I can't stand her."

"It's not her fault you didn't get the dagger," said Billy, but he shut the door. "Are you going to Suzy's birthday party?"

"I guess."

"What are you getting her?"

Paul knew that his mother had not bought Suzy's present yet.

Suddenly, he had an idea. "Maybe I could give her *Angus, Boy of Scotland*!" he said.

After lunch Paul brought the matter up with his mother.

"Suzy likes to read," he said. "I could give her my book, and then I could take the money you were going to spend on her present and buy a tarantula with it."

Paul's mother shivered. "Not a chance. I refuse to have a pet that shows up on an exterminator's list."

"Or a gerbil, maybe." Paul had not been very hopeful about the tarantula anyway, even if Billy had promised to take care of it when they were away on vacation.

"No, no gerbil, either. Not right now. I have my hands full as it is."

"I could get a couple of water pistols, I guess."

"You could get Suzy's birthday present is what you could get. I wish I had bought it before now. Hardly anything's open on Sunday. Do you want to go to the drugstore with me?"

"I bet she'd like my book better than anything you could buy at the old drugstore."

"No, Paul. The subject is closed. Granny's feelings would be hurt if you gave away the book."

Chapter Six

*P*aul took two boxes of pink stationery with little flowers to Suzy's party.

The Harts had hired a magician for the party. When Paul arrived the magician was standing by the picnic table doing tricks. Paul sat down on the grass to watch. The magician wore a tall black hat and a cape. He pulled a long line of colored scarves out of his sleeve. The children clapped. The magician took his hat off and showed everybody that it was empty. Next he pulled a rabbit out of the hat. It was not a real rabbit, though. It was a small toy rabbit. Paul was pretty sure it had been hidden in the magician's sleeve along with the scarves. Now if he had pulled a real live tarantula out of the hat, then they would have had something.

A lot of kids were at Suzy's party. Tiffany was there, too. Paul knew why. Suzy's mother had made her ask Tiffany. Paul had somebody like that at his birthday party, too—Melissa Grant. Paul had asked Mike Grant and his mother said he had to ask Melissa because Melissa was Mike's twin sister.

For his last trick, the magician made a toy chick appear behind Suzy's ear. Then he bowed and all the children clapped. The magician packed the toy rabbit and the scarves into a black briefcase.

After the magician left, everyone gathered around the picnic table to watch Suzy open her presents. She got two My Little Ponies, two gift certificates to bookstores, three puzzles, a lot of fluffy stuffed animals, a paint-by-numbers kit, a sticker book, and the stationery Paul had given her. Only one of her presents was interesting. Billy had given her a book, *200 Awesomely Tasteless Jokes.* "My mom let me buy the present all by myself," Billy whispered to Paul. "I got it gift wrapped for free."

When Mrs. Hart saw the book, she smiled

and took it into the house. Paul was pretty sure he could have gotten Suzy to trade that book for *Angus, Boy of Scotland*, if only his mother had let him.

Mr. Hart had been cooking hot dogs in the grill while Suzy opened the presents. Now he laid all the hot dogs on a big platter. Mrs. Hart began putting them in buns.

"Do you have any chili?" asked Heather Marks.

"No chili," said Mrs. Hart.

"I don't like onions," Billy said. "Don't put any onions on mine."

Mrs. Hart squeezed ketchup on a hot dog.

"Do you have any hamburgers? I don't like hot dogs," another kid said.

"Just hot dogs today," said Mrs. Hart. She sounded tense. "If you can't eat them, then you can fill up on the other food and birthday cake."

Paul could eat hot dogs any way. When he got his hot dog, he ate it right away and then asked for another one. Mrs. Hart seemed to have lost track of who had had hot dogs and who hadn't. Her hair was falling into her eyes as she kept handing out hot dogs.

The Harts' dog circled the picnic tables eating what the kids dropped on the ground. Some of the kids fed him parts of their hot dogs. He put his paws up on the table.

"Down, Boopsie," said Mr. Hart. "Get down from there."

Boopsie pawed at a paper plate until it fell down on the ground. Quickly, he gobbled up the piece of hot dog that had fallen off it.

"It's okay," said Amy Brown. "I was finished."

Mr. Hart made Boopsie go inside the house anyway.

When everybody was through eating, they sang "Happy Birthday" and Suzy blew out the candles on her cake. Mr. Hart took a picture. For a minute after that Paul saw blue spots in front of his eyes.

Mrs. Hart cut the cake and began handing out slices. "This is my favorite part," whispered Billy. Paul's slice had a rose on it. The good thing about roses was that they were made of icing. You couldn't have too much icing, in Paul's opinion. He finished his slice off in no time. Billy ate his quickly, too. Only a few crumbs were left on the boys' Snoopy plates.

Paul and Billy would have liked seconds, but after Mrs. Hart had cut a piece for everyone she picked the cake up and took it into the kitchen.

"I have room for another piece of cake," said Tiffany loudly. "Those were little pieces."

For once Paul agreed with Tiffany. They had been little pieces.

"I don't want anybody to get an upset stomach," said Mrs. Hart over her shoulder. "I think we'd better stop with just one piece."

When she got back Mrs. Hart collected all the dirty paper plates and began stuffing them in a plastic garbage can.

Paul decided he liked his birthday party better than Suzy's. Paul's father always gave everybody big pieces of cake. Also, Paul got better presents than Suzy. Nobody ever gave him fluffy stuffed animals or stationery. He got things like cars and monsters. One year Billy had even given him some slime made out of gooey plastic. Paul's mother hadn't taken it away to the kitchen, either.

While the Harts cleaned up, the kids started running around the big backyard. Three boys got on Suzy's sliding board, but Mr. Hart made them get off. "Only one at a time on the sliding board," he said. "We don't want any broken bones."

The best thing in Suzy's yard was the line with a sliding wheel mounted on it. Her father had strung it between two trees. Kids could grab onto the wheel at one end of the line, lift their legs off the ground, and have a long ride to the tree at the other end of the yard. "I'm Tarzan," Paul yelled, grabbing hold of the wheel. The trees whizzed by and the wind blew in his face as he held on tight. When he got to the other end of the yard he put his feet down. He turned around to see if anybody had noticed how fast he went. He wished Tiffany had seen what a good ride he had had, but she wasn't around.

"Bring it back," yelled Billy. "It's my turn now."

Paul walked back to the beginning of the line pulling the wheel along with him.

Billy grabbed hold of the wheel and took

off with a running start. He lifted his feet and rode to the other side of the yard.

Other kids came over to have turns. Paul sighed. Now he wished nobody had noticed what good rides he and Billy had had. He'd be lucky to have two more turns before the party was over.

After a while a white car drove up to the Harts' house. A mother got out and came through the gate to the backyard. She stood and talked to Suzy's mother. Three more cars pulled up in front of the house. More parents got out and came to the backyard to talk to the Harts. Paul saw that Mrs. Hart gave one of them a slice of birthday cake. There was plenty of birthday cake left. Mrs. Hart should have let them have more, Paul thought.

A couple of kids got in their parents' cars and rode away. Paul was glad his parents hadn't come yet. He was just about to get another turn on the ride. He saw a blue Plymouth drive up and Tiffany's parents got out of it. Paul looked around but he didn't see Tiffany. She was probably hiding. She sure was a pain.

"Hey, it's my turn!" Paul cried suddenly.

He had been so busy watching for Tiffany, he had almost let somebody get ahead of him. He grabbed hold of the wheel and took off.

When Paul's ride was over, he saw Mr. Davis over by the swing set. He was looking around. "Have you seen Tiffany, Paul?" he asked. Paul shook his head.

"Have you seen Tiffany, Suzy?"

Suzy shook her head and went on swinging.

Mr. Davis walked back to the group of grown-ups talking by the picnic table.

Mrs. Hart and Mr. Davis began walking together. "She has to be here somewhere," said Mrs. Hart. "With the fence around the yard, there's no way she could have wandered off. Tiffany!"

Paul wondered where Tiffany could be hiding.

"Billy, have you seen Tiffany?" asked Mrs. Hart.

Billy shook his head.

Paul was curious now. There were not too many places to hide in Suzy's yard. One time he had hidden behind the woodpile during hide-and-seek. He walked over to the wood pile, but Tiffany was not there.

"I know," said Mrs. Hart. "I bet she went inside to go to the bathroom. I should have thought of that. She'll probably be out again in a minute." The two grown-ups went into the house to check the bathrooms.

By now quite a few kids had gone home.

"You could have another turn now," Billy said. "David had to go home."

"I wonder where Tiffany is hiding," said Paul.

"Maybe she's been kidnapped," said Billy.

Paul did not like that idea. "That's stupid!" he said loudly. "How could anybody kidnap her with all these people here?"

Billy shrugged.

Mrs. Hart walked toward them and looked behind the woodpile. "I don't see how she could have climbed over the fence without anyone's noticing," she said.

"I think we had better search the house again," said Mr. Davis. "Paul, you come with me. We're going to go in the house and look for Tiffany."

"My mother is going to be picking me up pretty soon," said Paul.

"Mrs. Hart will tell her that you're helping me out. Come on."

Mrs. Davis squeezed her hands. "Where can she be? I wonder if we should call the police."

"She can't have gone far," said Mrs. Hart. "Jim and I were here the whole time. We're probably overlooking something very obvious."

"Tif-fany!" yelled Mrs. Davis.

"Tiffany!" shouted Billy.

Paul did not hurry to follow Mr. Davis. He figured he would feel stupid searching for Tiffany. If he found her, she would just laugh at him. He had never known anybody in his whole life who was such a pain.

"Oh, my goodness," said Mrs. Hart suddenly. "You don't think she could have gotten into the crawl space under the house!"

The two women ran over to the house. Mrs. Hart opened the trapdoor at the base of the house. "Jim!" she yelled. "Bring me a flashlight."

This was beginning to get interesting, Paul thought. What if Tiffany had crawled under the house? Mrs. Hart was going to have a fit if she had.

Just then Paul saw Tiffany slide down out of the tree near the swing. His mouth dropped open. Nobody had thought to look up among the leaves for Tiffany.

"Mom!" Suzy shrieked. "There she is! Tiffany's not lost. She's right here!"

Mrs. Hart and Mrs. Davis hurried over to Tiffany. Mrs. Davis hugged her tight. "Where were you, Tiff? We looked and looked! Why did you give us a scare like that?"

"I was just climbing a tree."

"Suzy," said Mrs. Hart. "Go in the house and tell Tiffany's dad that we found her."

"Didn't you hear us?" asked Mrs. Davis. "We went all over the yard calling for you!"

"I was playing hide-and-seek."

"You frightened us, Tiffany," said Mrs. Davis. "You mustn't do that. We were afraid you were hurt or lost."

"It was just a game."

"Well, it wasn't a very good game," said Mrs. Davis. "I'm terribly sorry about all this trouble, Christine."

Mrs. Hart gave a weak smile. "I'm just glad we found her."

"That Tiffany is so stupid," Paul told Suzy. "Why did she want to hide like that?"

"She's lucky they didn't call the police," said Suzy.

Paul thought about that. If they had called the police there might have been sirens and crackling radios like in the movies. Also, everybody would have been really mad at Tiffany then. It was too bad, he decided, that she had come out of hiding so soon.

Chapter Seven

Mrs. Fenner taped a piece of masking tape to a soft drink can. She wrote Paul's name on it. "Give this to Mrs. Warren as soon as you get there so she can put it in the cooler," she said. "It's not cold now, but it will be by lunchtime."

"I know that," Paul said. "I'm the one who told you." Paul thought field trips made his mother jumpy. She didn't usually say such dumb things.

"Here's your lunch."

Paul peeked inside the bag to make sure it was something he liked. He was glad to smell peanut butter.

"I'm going to give you five dollars in case you want to buy a souvenir."

46

"Aw-right!"

"Just don't lose it. Do you want me to pin it in your pocket with a safety pin?"

"I'm not going to lose it. Jeez, Mom!"

A horn honked outside. Mrs. Fenner kissed Paul good-bye. "Okay, sweetheart, have a good time!"

"No problem!" crowed Paul as he went out the door. He loved field trips.

Paul and Billy always sat together on the bus. They planned it that way so they wouldn't get stuck sitting next to somebody they didn't like. This was particularly important because both the second and third grades were going to the science museum. Paul was afraid Tiffany might sit with him. Most girls wouldn't sit next to a boy, but Paul felt he couldn't count on Tiffany to act like most girls. He didn't feel safe until he and Billy were on the bus. "Phew," said Paul. "That was a close call." Tiffany sat down in the seat behind them.

Paul heard the sound of paper crackling and turned around. Tiffany was peeking inside her lunch bag. She wrinkled up her nose. "I hate pimento cheese," she said.

Mrs. Warren stood at the front of the bus. "All right, boys and girls, I want you to be on your best behavior when we get to the museum. Remember that you represent Fuller Elementary School. When the bus starts, you may talk quietly or you may sing together, if you wish. You may *not* sing 'Ninety-nine Bottles of Beer on the Wall.' "

"Why not?" asked Paul.

The bus took off with a roar.

Paul settled back in his seat. "Have you ever been to the science museum before?" he asked.

"I don't think so," said Billy.

"It's neat. I hope they let us buy souvenirs. That's the best part. When I went with my dad I got a piece of fool's gold. I don't know what I'm going to get this time, but something good. My mom gave me five dollars."

"I've got two dollars. You think I can get a souvenir with that?"

"Sure. They have all kinds of things there. Postcards. Sharks' teeth."

"Sharks' teeth? Hey, aw-right!"

"My mother gave me some money, too," said Tiffany loudly.

"You can buy a souvenir, too," said Billy.

"Ignore her," whispered Paul.

The bus pulled into a parking space in front of the museum. Across the street was a Burger King. Tiffany stood up and pressed her nose against the window so she could see the Burger King better. "Aw-right!" she said.

Mrs. Warren stood at the front of the bus. "Sit down, until I tell you," she said, staring at Tiffany.

Tiffany sat down and Mrs. Warren went on talking. "There will be no hitting or shoving, boys or girls. If anybody misbehaves he or she will have to go out to the bus and wait with the bus driver. That person will miss out on seeing the museum. We will eat our lunches in the museum garden. I want you to be very careful not to be litterbugs. Be sure to put your bags and papers in the trash can. And remember, the most important thing is to stay together. It's a big museum."

As the class got off the bus Paul caught the smell of french fries coming from across the street at the Burger King. Paul figured Tiffany smelled it, too, because she was smiling.

49

Inside the museum a pretty lady with long blond hair met them. "Hi, kids. My name is Mandy. The first thing we are going to visit is the dinosaur room."

The lady led them into a big room. Inside was a *Brontosaurus* skeleton. It was huge. It looked bigger than a house.

"Wow!" said Paul.

"Don't touch!" said Mrs. Warren.

"If you look up," said their guide, "you can see the skeleton of a killer whale and next to it the skeleton of a blue whale. They are hanging from wires on the ceiling."

The room was painted black so they could easily see the white bones against the walls. Paul was surprised that the killer whale was smaller than the other one. He remembered that the *Tyrannosaurus,* the killer dinosaur, was smaller than the plant-eating *Brontosaurus.* Paul turned to Tiffany. Being big isn't everything, he thought.

The best part of the museum came just before lunch. The children went into a room where jungle plants grew behind a big sheet of glass.

"Take your seats, boys and girls, and I will introduce you to Curly," said the guide.

A man came out with a giant python coiled around his back and his arms.

"Oooo," said the children.

Paul bounced up and down in his seat. "How do you know he won't squeeze you?" he yelled.

The man smiled. "He won't squeeze me because he's not hungry. Also, he's used to people."

"What do you feed him?" asked Billy.

"Live rats."

Suzy's hand went up in front of her mouth. Her eyes were big.

The pretty guide clapped her hands. "We need a volunteer. Who would like to come up to pet Curly?"

Almost every child put his or her hand up.

"Me! Me!" they shouted.

Paul noticed that Suzy did not have her hand up.

The lady chose Billy to pet the python.

"Lu-cky!" said Paul.

Paul heard a funny sound. Tiffany's stomach was growling loudly. Paul was hungry,

too. It was almost time for lunch. He was glad
he had a peanut butter sandwich for lunch and
not pimento cheese like Tiffany.

"All right, boys and girls. Curly has to take
his nap now." The pretty lady smiled. "And
you get to eat your lunches."

Mrs. Warren led the children to the museum garden. When everyone had found a
place to sit, she began passing out drinks.

"Where's Tiffany?" asked Billy.

"Who cares?" said Paul. He unwrapped his
sandwich and took a bite of it.

"She was right next to you when we were
in the snake room," said Billy. "I heard her
stomach growling. Now I don't see her
anywhere."

Paul looked around. Tiffany was tall and
her hair was very blond. She was not easy to
miss. Paul did not see her anywhere, either.

"Maybe Curly ate her for lunch." He cov-
ered his mouth and laughed.

"That's not funny, Paul," said Suzy.

"She's probably hiding again," said Billy.

"Maybe we ought to tell Mrs. Warren,"
said Suzy.

"It doesn't have anything to do with us," said Paul.

Paul ate his sandwich. Suzy ate only half of hers. "You don't want the rest of that sandwich?" asked Paul. He thought he might have room for the other half of Suzy's sandwich.

Suddenly a police officer came out into the garden. He was holding Tiffany's hand. Mrs. Torres, Tiffany's teacher, turned white when she saw Tiffany with the officer. Tiffany was holding a bag of french fries.

"Lost anybody?" asked the officer. He pushed his cap back on his head and smiled at the teachers.

"Tiffany!" said Mrs. Torres.

Mrs. Warren stood up. "Boys and girls," she said, "those of you who have finished lunch may now come with me to the museum shop."

The children followed Mrs. Warren back into the museum.

"She doesn't want us to know why Tiffany got arrested," said Paul.

"What do you think she did?" asked Billy.

"Maybe she robbed a bank. It wouldn't surprise me if she did. Boy, is she in trouble."

"She's always in trouble," said Suzy. "When Kate had her slumber party she went outside. We all looked everywhere for her. I even looked in the bathtub, but she wasn't there. She was out on the deck. Mr. Gray found her and then he took her home. Now she can't go over to Kate's house anymore. Kate's mom said she couldn't."

"Who cares?" asked Paul.

"Kate only asked her to her party because her mother made her," said Suzy.

Paul wished she would quit talking about Tiffany. People talked about Tiffany too much. He went over to check out the museum shop's books.

The museum shop had so many great things that Paul could not make up his mind. He saw a book on pythons with a lot of pictures. Also, there were rock samples and lots of different models of dinosaurs.

"I'm going to get a shark's tooth," said Billy. "It doesn't cost too much. I'll have some money left over."

Paul was worried. Soon Mrs. Warren would say it was time to go. He still hadn't made up his mind.

"Boys and girls," said Mrs. Warren, "you should take your souvenirs to the cash register now. We have to be going."

Paul panicked. He hadn't chosen anything yet.

Billy was already standing in line by the cash register. He was holding a small shark's tooth in a clear plastic envelope.

Suddenly Paul saw what he wanted. A fat envelope was displayed near the cash register. "Genuine rattlesnake eggs," the envelope said. "Store in a cool place."

Paul watched carefully while Billy paid for his shark's tooth. He was glad that the lady at the cash register was not one of those who announced each purchase. At the fruit market where Paul's mother shopped, the man at the counter would say, "One pound of bananas at sixty-nine cents a pound," when he rang up the bill. Paul knew that if the lady at the cash register said, "One package of rattlesnake eggs at three dollars and fifty cents," it would catch Mrs. Warren's attention pretty quick.

Paul slid his five-dollar bill across the counter. The lady at the cash register rang up the price. Then she put Paul's envelope of eggs in a paper bag. The paper bag had a picture of a dinosaur on it. Paul breathed a sigh of relief. His eggs were hidden now.

"I can't make up my mind," said Jason Hardy.

"You must complete your purchases, boys and girls," said Mrs. Warren. "We have to be going."

Jason Hardy quickly bought a model of a dinosaur.

When the class walked back to the bus, Paul held his bag out away from the warmth of his body. He didn't want the eggs to hatch too soon.

Chapter
Eight

When Paul got home after school, he got out his old goldfish bowl. Over its top he put a piece of net from his mother's box of sewing scraps. He put a rubber band around the top so the net would not come off.

The package said, "Keep cool." So, if he wanted to hatch the eggs, he figured, all he had to do was get them warm. It was easy. Paul got a heating pad from the hall closet. His dad used the heating pad when his back hurt. Paul put the heating pad on the floor of his closet. He turned the heating pad's dial to LOW. He was afraid if it was too hot it might cook his eggs. He poured the leathery eggs into the goldfish bowl. Next he set the goldfish bowl on top of the heating pad. He carefully shut his closet door. What a great thing this was going to be to take to show-and-tell—fifteen baby rattlesnakes!

The next day was Saturday. Paul asked his father to take him to the library. He wanted to find out how long it would take his snake eggs to hatch.

"It's nice to see you taking such an interest in reading," his father said, pleased.

When they came back from the library Paul read the books on snakes in the car on the way home. The books had the same old stuff that he already knew. Snakes are reptiles. They help the farmer by eating rats. None of the books said how long it took rattlesnakes to hatch.

"These books don't have any of the good stuff," Paul said. "They just have dumb stuff I already know."

"Next time we'll go over to the adult section," said Paul's dad. "You can probably get a more in-depth treatment there. What are you looking for?"

"Just stuff," said Paul.

When they got home, Paul could hear Tiffany's mom's voice coming from the kitchen.

"We could be swept away by a tornado and I don't think that child would turn a hair. Haven't you noticed? She's perfectly friendly to us, but she's friendly to everybody. We're nothing special to her. It's not the way I thought it would be at all."

"She just needs time to settle in," said Paul's mother.

"She's been settling in for months." Mrs. Davis sighed. "They say she's so ahead that she really should be moved up a grade. She reads on a fifth-grade level. But I wonder if Glenda Torres isn't just passing the buck."

"Honey, we're home," Paul's dad called.

"I'd better be going," said Mrs. Davis.

After she left, Paul said, "What did she want?"

"I asked her in for a cup of coffee," said Paul's mom.

"Yeah, but what was she talking about?"

"Oh, nothing much. They may move Tiffany up a grade."

"Oh, no! What if she ends up in my room!"

"What if she does?"

"That'll be pretty bad. That's all," Paul said darkly.

He went to look in his closet and check on his rattlesnake eggs. So far none of them had hatched.

"Paul," said his mother. She was standing at his door. "What is that light?"

The heating pad dial had a small light that lit up when it was turned on.

"Nothing," said Paul. He smiled at her and closed the closet door.

"Paul Alexander Fenner, what are you up to?" His mother opened the closet. "What is a goldfish bowl doing in your closet? And why do you have Daddy's heating pad?"

Paul sighed. "I'm just hatching my rattle-snake eggs."

Paul's mother screamed

His father ran in. "Paul is hatching rattle-snake eggs," Mrs. Fenner said. She quickly turned off the heating pad.

"Don't do that," said Paul. "You have to keep them warm to hatch them."

"That's what I thought," said Mrs. Fenner.

"Are you sure they're real?" asked Mr. Fenner.

"I got them from the science museum," said Paul.

"The science museum trip was only two days ago, Emmy. They can't be ready to hatch yet. Let's just calm down," said Mr. Fenner.

"I am calm," said Mrs. Fenner. "I'm as calm as a woman can be with rattlesnakes in her son's bedroom."

Mrs. Fenner carried the goldfish bowl into the kitchen. She held the goldfish bowl away from her as if it might explode. When she got to the kitchen she put the goldfish bowl in the freezer and slammed the door shut.

"That's a good idea," said Mr. Fenner. "Once they're frozen we know they won't hatch."

"Murderer," said Paul.

Mr. Fenner read to Paul out of the snake book they got from the library. He read very loudly when he got to the part that said, "Baby snakes are venomous as soon as they are hatched." Mr. Fenner believed anything could be turned into an educational experience.

Paul did not see what his mother and father were so excited about. He had put the eggs in a goldfish bowl so they couldn't get out, hadn't he?

Monday Paul took his rattlesnake eggs to show-and-tell. He explained that since they had been frozen they could not hatch. Mrs. Warren looked happy to hear it.

After show-and-tell, Mrs. Warren said, "Class, we have a new student today."

Paul was not surprised that the new student was Tiffany.

"Hi, Paul," said Tiffany.

"Oh, you already know some of the children in the class," said Mrs. Warren. "That's good."

Tiffany was put in the first reading group.

"It figures," said Paul. First his rattlesnake eggs had gotten frozen and now this.

Chapter
Nine

*B*oys and girls," said Mrs. Warren, "the second week in February is National Dental Health Week. Each of you will be given a package of dental floss. We plan to celebrate Dental Health Week by flossing our teeth every day. Dr. Horace Cooley will visit us next Wednesday and talk to us about good dental health habits."

"Next Wednesday is Valentine's Day," said Billy. He knew because he was thinking of sending a valentine to Suzy. Maybe.

"You know what Dental Health Week means?" said Paul. "It means no candy on Valentine's Day."

"No!" said Billy.

"I bet you," said Paul.

Usually the mothers brought cookies and candy on special occasions. At Christmas they brought Christmas cookies and candy canes. At Easter time they brought candy Easter eggs and cupcakes with yellow chicks on top. Last year for Valentine's Day they had brought pink punch and heart-shaped candy.

Paul raised his hand. "What about Valentine's Day?"

"I'm glad you asked," said Mrs. Warren. "I almost forgot the most important part. On Valentine's Day we will present a puppet show about dental health. We will start making our puppets tomorrow. Each of you should bring a balloon and some old newspapers."

"Is that all?" asked Paul.

"The school will provide the paste and the paints," said Mrs. Warren. "And I will bring some boxes from home."

"I mean, is that all we're going to do on Valentine's Day?" asked Paul.

"We will have a very busy day with Dr. Cooley and the puppet show. I don't think we will have time to exchange valentine cards."

"What about valentine candy?" asked Billy.

"Candy is not in keeping with the spirit of National Dental Health Week," said Mrs. Warren. "We all know that candy is not good for teeth. Now, boys and girls, please remember to bring your newspaper and your balloon tomorrow. We must get to work right away on the puppets. If we practice hard we will get to put on our puppet show for Mrs. Torres's class."

"I like candy better," whispered Billy.

Paul had to agree.

The next day Mrs. Warren put out the newspapers the children brought. She put out bowls of flour-and-water paste, too.

"We are going to need a lot of strong, healthy teeth puppets," she said.

Paul knew that everybody who didn't get to be something interesting would be stuck being a strong healthy tooth.

Mrs. Warren cast Suzy as the toothbrush. Lib Taylor was to be a lollipop.

"Your puppet will look like you," said Tiffany. "You're round like a lollipop."

Lib burst into tears.

"Tiffany hurt Lib's feelings," Suzy told Mrs. Warren. "She said Lib was fat."

"I just said she was round like a lollipop. She is."

"Tiffany, come up here and sit by me until I finish casting," said Mrs. Warren.

Paul waited while Mrs. Warren cast Mike Pitts as a tube of toothpaste, Michelle Langley as an apple, and Alvin Cooper as a carton of milk. Paul just knew he was going to be stuck being a healthy tooth. He remembered the Christmas pageant at church when he was part of the heavenly host and had to wear those dumb wings. "If I just had a speaking part!" he had told his mother then. "Or if I could be one of the wise men! I wouldn't care even if all I did was hold the star! But being one of the heavenly host stinks." The puppet show was going to be just like the Christmas pageant.

Mrs. Warren began telling people that they were going to be strong healthy teeth. Paul looked down at his desk. When it came time for the play, he would just stay home from school. He would have a stomachache. It was a waste of time being a strong, healthy tooth.

He would rather stay home and watch "The Young and the Restless."

"I don't want to be a tooth," said Robert Bryant. "They don't get to say anything."

"The strong, healthy teeth are an important part of the show," said Mrs. Warren. "Remember, Robert, there are no small parts. There are only small actors."

Everyone stared at her in disbelief.

Paul realized that almost everybody had a part by now. Maybe Mrs. Warren would forget him.

"Now for the part of Mr. Tooth Decay," said Mrs. Warren.

Paul sat up straight. He was the only boy left who did not have a part. He knew Mrs. Warren would not give the part to Robert Bryant because Robert had complained. That was the way Mrs. Warren was.

Paul sat very still. He even held his breath. He was afraid he might do something that would keep Mrs. Warren from making him Mr. Tooth Decay. Paul was already imagining the black puppet he would make. What a part! This would be even better than holding the star in the Christmas pageant.

"Wait a minute," said Tiffany. "Why do we have to have a Mr. Tooth Decay? Why can't we have a Miss Tooth Decay?"

Paul shot her a nasty look.

"She's right," said Suzy. "It's not fair."

Paul felt betrayed. Suzy was his friend.

Mrs. Warren hesitated. "I guess it's true that tooth decay could be either Mr. or Miss," she said. "Would one of the girls like to be Miss Tooth Decay?"

Suzy and Tiffany both put their hands high in the air.

Paul slumped in his seat. He knew he would never get to be Mr. Tooth Decay now. "People who complain never get picked," he said to Tiffany.

"Complaining is not the same as pointing out an injustice," Tiffany said.

Paul glared at her. If his eyes had been laser beams, she would have burst into flames. It was so unfair that Tiffany was tall and that she knew words like *injustice*.

Mrs. Warren hesitated. Tiffany was not a favorite of hers, but she prided herself on being fair. It had been Tiffany who had no-

69

ticed the sexism in the casting of tooth decay. "All right," she said. "Tiffany can be Miss Tooth Decay."

Paul tried to act as if he didn't care that he was going to be a healthy tooth. It wasn't easy.

Chapter
Ten

During the rehearsal for the puppet show, Tiffany told Suzy that she should have been the candy. "You're so sweet you make me sick," said Tiffany.

"Why do you have to be so mean?" asked Suzy.

That afternoon Suzy passed around a petition. "Will everyone who has been insulted by Tiffany Davis or had their feelings hurt by her please sign this petition?"

Suzy was the first person who signed it. When it got to Paul, four other people had added their names under Suzy's. Paul did not sign it. He did not like to admit that Tiffany got to him. He passed it back to Carlos. Carlos was not paying much attention. He saw

Tiffany's name at the top of the note and passed it across the aisle to Tiffany.

"What's this?" said Mrs. Warren. She took the petition from Tiffany.

Paul knew that Suzy had made a mistake to put her name first. Now it would be easy for Mrs. Warren to tell who had started the petition.

"Suzy," said Mrs. Warren. "I think you and I had better have a little talk after school today."

Suzy turned red. She had never had to stay after school in her life.

Paul whispered, "Don't worry, Suzy. I'll tell the car pool to wait."

"Don't speak to me, Paul Fenner," Suzy whispered back.

Paul glanced at Billy and shrugged.

When Paul's mother came home after work, he told her that his stomach hurt. He was practicing for Valentine's Day. She put her hand on his forehead. "You don't feel warm." She seemed to be worried. "Do you feel like eating supper?"

Paul shrugged. "It comes and goes," he said.

Paul ate a double helping of spaghetti at supper. After supper Paul could hear his parents talking in the kitchen. His mother sounded upset so Paul stood outside the door and listened. He thought maybe they were talking about his stomachache.

"I don't know how they can live with themselves," said Mrs. Fenner. "That helpless little child. How can they call themselves parents? How can they call themselves human beings?" Paul heard a pot crashing against a pot.

"Calm down," said Mr. Fenner. "You're going to break something."

"She said the agency should have told them how many foster homes Tiffany had been in. I told her that the agency didn't even *know*. We only got Tiffany's records later. What difference does that make? The more foster homes Tiffany was in the more she needed a really good permanent home. I couldn't say that, of course. It was clear the woman had made up her mind."

"You're taking this too personally," said Mr. Fenner. "They obviously aren't the right family for a child with special needs."

"But after we told Tiffany this was her family, after we told her that this time she was there for keeps!"

"It's bad all right."

"I can't look the woman in the face. I'm so mad I want to spit. It's awful that they're right here in the neighborhood."

"What are you going to do?"

"We're going to get Tiffany in therapy, first. We don't usually have money for it, but I told Alice the agency had to find the money somewhere and she agreed. We have a responsibility to Tiffany."

"Then what?"

"Well, if she were a little older, we'd put her in a foster home, but since she's so young, we're going to make another try at adoption." Mrs. Fenner gave a tired sigh. "This time it's got to be absolutely right. We're not going to take any chances. We can't afford another mistake."

"The poor kid."

"Right now, of course, we're all just in shock."

Paul felt short of breath. He could tell something awful had happened to Tiffany, but

he couldn't figure out what exactly. He tiptoed away from the kitchen door. Then he
remembered that he was being just like Tiffany. He was spying! It made him feel cold all
over when he thought of that.

That night when his mother tucked him in,
he had a real stomachache. "I hurt here," he
said, putting his hand on his stomach.

"Too much spaghetti, I'll bet," said his
mother.

"I need another kiss," said Paul.

"All right, but then I have to go, sweetheart. I brought work home."

After Paul's mother left the room, the
darkness felt scary. Paul wished he had not
listened to what his mom and dad were saying in the kitchen. He didn't feel sick from
too much spaghetti. He felt sick from worrying about Tiffany. His back was stiff and
he could feel the sweat on it. His toe itched.
He could not get comfortable no matter how
he twisted around in the bedclothes. He
stared at the ceiling a long time, unable to
close his eyes.

★   ★   ★

The next morning the car pool didn't pick up Tiffany. Paul panicked. "What about Tiffany?" he said. "You forgot her."

Mrs. Hart seemed to be uncomfortable. "We're not picking up Tiffany this morning," she said.

"Why not?" said Paul. "Is she sick or something?"

"She's moving."

"I didn't see any moving truck," said Paul.

Suzy kicked the back of the front seat angrily. "I don't see why everybody's acting so weird. Tiffany, Tiffany. Everybody keeps talking about Tiffany. Who cares about Tiffany?"

"Susan, I've told you a hundred times not to kick the seat," her mother said angrily. "Now, would you please settle down. I have to concentrate on driving."

"Tiffany's going to live with a new family," Suzy told Paul. "My mother already told me about it."

Paul's eyes were wide. "But she was chosen by the Davises. They can't just give her away, can they?"

"The Davises weren't the right family for

her," said Mrs. Hart. She accidentally bumped her elbow against the horn. Paul jumped at the noise. "Now, see what you kids made me do," said Mrs. Hart. "I don't know if I'm coming or going."

"Tiffany was crazy," said Suzy. "That's why they gave her away. She was weird."

"That's not true," said Paul.

"Suzy," said her mother, "you don't know anything about it. Why don't you be quiet? It's very sad and very upsetting for us all, but I'm afraid there's nothing we can do."

"Watch out!" said Paul.

"Be quiet, Paul!"

"You just ran a red light," Paul pointed out. "I thought you'd want to know."

Suzy's mom pressed her hand to her head. "We are all going to have to be quiet or I am going to wreck the car. Is that understood?"

"Yes, ma'am," said Suzy. She folded her hands in her lap. Paul and Suzy were quiet the rest of the way to school.

At school when Mrs. Warren called roll, she didn't call Tiffany's name.

"You forgot Tiffany," said Paul.

"I didn't forget Tiffany," Mrs. Warren said

quietly. "I didn't call her name because she has moved. She is transferring to a new school district."

Mrs. Warren passed out the paper for the spelling test. She didn't say anything more about Tiffany, but Paul noticed that she looked sad.

At recess Paul said to Suzy, "Don't you think it's funny about Tiffany? The way she just disappeared like that? It's like on this movie I saw one time. This kid was in a shopping center and then this flying saucer came and got him and nobody ever saw him again."

Paul had not seen a movie like that. He was making it up. He couldn't quit thinking about the way Tiffany had just disappeared, but he didn't want to come right out and say so. Making up the story about the movie was a way for him to talk about it. Paul wondered if anybody else was worrying about Tiffany. Didn't they realize that if she could be un-adopted like that, it could happen to any of them? It could even happen to him. Paul gulped. His stomach was feeling strange again.

"I'm glad she's gone," said Suzy. Paul noticed that she was sucking her thumb. He remembered that Suzy used to suck her thumb before first grade. He hadn't seen her do it in a long time.

"She was real bad," said Paul. "That's probably why they got rid of her. Remember how she got arrested when we went to the museum?"

"That's what I said," said Suzy.

"She was smart, though," said Paul.

Suzy didn't say anything. They both knew Tiffany was smart.

"I wish I knew what really happened," Paul said.

"It doesn't have anything to do with us," said Suzy.

"I know. I'd just like to know, that's all," said Paul.

That night Paul's mother tucked him in. "Be sure and set my alarm," he said. "I want to get up by myself."

Mrs. Fenner smiled. "My Paul is getting so grown-up."

Paul waited until his mother had left. Then he took his pillow and blanket and crawled under the bed with them. If a burglar got into the house, Paul knew he would never think to look under the bed. The dust in the box springs made him feel sneezy, but he felt safer under the bed. He was going to do his best to make sure he did not disappear like Tiffany.

Chapter
Eleven

At school the children were working on their puppets.

"Since Tiffany has gone to a new school, we need someone else to be Miss Tooth Decay," said Mrs. Warren. "What about you, Suzy?"

Suzy took a step backward. "I'd rather be a strong, healthy tooth," she said.

"Well, Tooth Decay doesn't have to be a girl," said Mrs. Warren. "It could be either a boy or a girl. Paul, didn't you want to be Tooth Decay? I know you have already started on your puppet, but if you paint it black instead of white, it would be a good Mr. Tooth Decay."

"No!" said Paul. He corrected himself carefully, "I mean, no, thank you."

So Carlos was Mr. Tooth Decay.

"I think he did a rotten job," Paul told his
mother after the show. "Rotten, heh-heh. Get
it?"

"I get it, Paul." His mother smiled.

"After Valentine's Day, there isn't another
holiday for a long time," said Paul. "And Valentine's Day was pretty much of a bust."

"There's April Fool's Day," said his
mother. "You like that."

Paul remembered when he had put a sack
of flour on top of the door to the kitchen.
When his dad opened the door the bag of flour
had fallen down and split open. Flour got all
over the kitchen. Even the cabinets got spat-
tered with flour. "April Fool!" Paul had
shouted.

"I'll April Fool you!" said his dad, but he
had laughed.

Thinking about it now, Paul did not think
it was funny. He would probably not do anything at all this coming April Fool's Day. He
did not want to do anything that was even a

little bit bad. Tiffany had been bad and look what had happened to her. Paul felt sick every time he thought about it.

"Do you know where Tiffany is?" he asked his mother.

"Of course, I know, sweetheart. She's living with a very nice family named Bonner."

"Maybe I could go see her."

"I didn't know you and Tiffany were friends. You were always complaining about her."

His mother was right. If he went to see Tiffany, what would he say to her? "Oh, well, forget it," he said.

For supper his mother fixed chicken breasts with Swiss cheese sauce.

Mr. Fenner pushed the chicken with his fork. "The sauce is kind of lumpy. Is that the way it's supposed to be?"

"I guess it was too hot when I put the cheese in," said Mrs. Fenner. "I don't fix a recipe this fancy very often. I need to do it again to get the bugs out of it."

Paul stuck out his tongue. "Bugs, yech."

"Paul, there aren't actually any bugs in the

sauce. That's just an expression. Why don't you taste it?"

"I'm not hungry," said Paul. He pushed his chair away from the table. "May I be excused?"

Paul's mother frowned as he left the table.

Paul went to his room and took out his stamp collection, but he couldn't keep his mind on it. He wished he could stop thinking about Tiffany. He thought about her more than when she was living right down the street and bugging him all the time. Thinking about her now, he shivered and slapped his stamp album closed.

Chapter
Twelve

One day Paul told his mother he was going to write a letter to Tiffany. Mrs. Fenner was a little puzzled. "That's nice," she said. "Everybody likes to get letters."

"You have her address, don't you, Mom?" Paul asked anxiously. "You said you knew where she was."

"Yes, I can get her address."

Paul wrote,

Dear Tiffany,
    Don't you miss your mom and your dad. Don't you miss your room and your toys. Don't you feel like crying all the time.

Paul

Mrs. Fenner read the letter. "Tiffany took her toys with her, Paul."

Paul neatly crossed out toys. "Now all I need to get is her address," he said.

"It's nice of you to write Tiffany, Paul, but don't you think you had better write a more cheerful letter?"

"You mean start all over?"

"Yes," said Mrs. Fenner.

"I could put in something cheerful in the P.S."

"I think you'd better start all over."

"Jeez," said Paul. "It's a lot of work to write a letter, you know."

"You could write about what is going on at school. Maybe you could think of something funny."

"Jeff Flynt fell off the sliding board and broke his arm."

"I don't think that's quite what you need."

Paul thought a minute. After a while he wrote,

Dear Tiffany,
    Carlos was Mr. tooth dekay. He was awful.

                                    Paul
P.S. I hope you like your new house.

88

"That's better," said Mrs. Fenner. "I know Tiffany will be very glad to get it. I'll mail it myself."

"I just hope she gets it," said Paul.

"Of course she'll get it."

Paul had the uncomfortable feeling that maybe his letter would disappear the way Tiffany had. He imagined his mother dropping it into one of the big mailboxes. Only his mom didn't realize that the box was really a cover-up for a deep hole that went down into the center of the earth. Paul figured that must be what happened to letters that ended up in the dead letter office. Paul wasn't sure what the dead letter office was, but it sounded like the end of everything. He hoped Tiffany was not at some place like the dead letter office.

The next day was Saturday. Paul drove into town with his mother to run errands. "I just have one more thing to get," she said. "Wood screws."

"I want to wait in the car," said Paul. He felt too tired to go into the hardware store. He felt tired a lot lately. Maybe he was wearing himself out with worry. It was tough always tensing up, waiting to disappear. Also he worried a lot about being good and about trapdoors and chutes to the center of the earth and stuff. Especially, he worried that his parents might move away and not tell him where they were going. It wasn't that he actually thought this was going to happen. It was just that he couldn't stop thinking about it. Especially at night. He almost couldn't think of anything else, then. When he thought about it, especially in the daytime, he realized it didn't make much sense. Why would his parents move away? It was more a feeling than a thought—a feeling that things could easily go very wrong.

"I guess you can stay in the car," said his mother. "I'll just be a minute. Lock the doors."

Mrs. Fenner went into the hardware store. The street was full of traffic. Many people did their shopping on Saturday. Across the street was a tobacco store. Paul noticed that it had a real cigar store Indian. He had never seen it before. It must be new. Paul stared at it so hard that after a minute his eyes felt dry. Staring at that Indian was the first thing that made him able to push away his fear. Suddenly he leapt out of the car and started across the street. He had to see the Indian up close. Brakes squealed. A pickup truck stopped inches from him. A station wagon thudded against the bumper of a Volvo. Paul looked around, bewildered. He had forgotten to notice the traffic. His mind was too full.

"Paul!" His mother screamed.

The man in the pickup shook his fist at Paul. "You want to die, kid?" he yelled. "Just keep it up!"

Paul darted between the cars. He was out of breath when he got to the cigar store Indian but he hadn't been hit by a car.

His mother ran up to the corner and crossed at the light. "Paul Alexander Fenner," she yelled. "What possessed you? You didn't look."

Paul blinked at her. He was having trouble getting his thoughts together. The cigar store Indian was all mixed up in his head with Tiffany.

"You could have been squashed flatter than a pancake," his mother yelled. "Don't you ever scare me like that again!"

Mrs. Fenner did not talk much on the way home, but Paul hardly noticed her silence. He felt tired again. He looked out the window of the car and thought about Tiffany. Paul tried hard not to think about Tiffany, but he couldn't stop himself. His mind was going in circles, but it didn't seem to get him anywhere.

That night Paul heard his parents talking in the kitchen. Even though Paul knew it was sneaky to tiptoe up to the door and listen to them, he had to do it. He could not stop himself. He wanted to be sure he would have some warning if something awful were about to happen to him. He didn't want to be caught by surprise like Tiffany.

"I'm worried about Paul," his mother said. "How could he jump out in traffic like that?"

"He just forgot to look, honey. He's never been one to think ahead. Remember the rattlesnake eggs?" Mr. Fenner laughed.

"This is different, I tell you. He's not having fun. He's not himself. He's been this way ever since Tiffany left."

"Well, that's been tough on everybody. Maybe we'd better talk to him."

Paul caught his breath. He was afraid they would get up right then to talk to him. They would catch him spying and be really mad. It was a scary thought. He tiptoed very quietly away from the kitchen. He went into his room and took out his stamp collection.

Soon his mother came in the room. "Paul," she said, "would you like to go visit Tiffany? I think I could arrange it."

Paul shook his head.

"The Davises weren't the right family for Tiffany, Paul. They expected too much from her. They expected her to be just like Jeff. It wasn't a good match. Now she's with a family that thinks she's terrific. Carolyn Winter, Tiffany's social worker, saw her just last week and she says Tiffany's never been happier. Believe me, sweetheart, it's been tough, but it's all working out."

Paul did not say anything. He licked a hinge and put it on a stamp. Then he stuck the stamp in his album.

Paul's mother sat down beside him on the floor. She put her arms around him. "We're

94

the right family for you, Pauley. We always have been. We always will be. Nothing will ever change that. You are our little boy. Do you hear what I'm saying?"

He nodded.

"Good." She hugged him tightly. "Are you about ready to go to bed now? I can tuck you in."

Paul's throat hurt. It didn't hurt the way it did when he had to go to the doctor and gargle with warm salt water. It felt as if it had a large sad lump in it so that he couldn't swallow. Paul was afraid that he was about to cry.

"I want to read the story of *The Runaway Bunny,*" he said gruffly.

"That's up in the attic," Mrs. Fenner said. "Remember when I put a lot of your baby books up in the attic?"

"I wish you hadn't put it up in the attic."

His mother thought a minute. "I'll go up and get it," she said.

Paul could hear his mother getting out the ladder to climb into the attic. After a while she came back. She blew the dust off the book. Paul sneezed.

Mrs. Fenner sat on the edge of the bed and

opened the book. Paul was already starting to feel better. It cheered him up to see the picture of the little bunny and his bunny mother in the book. "If you run away," read Mrs. Fenner, "I will run after you. For you are my little bunny."

"I like the part where he changes into a fish and she fishes for him," said Paul quickly. "And the part where he gets wings and the mamma bunny turns into a tree for him to land in."

"I believe you know this story by heart," teased Mrs. Fenner.

"Go on," said Paul. He was holding on to the satin edge of his blanket. It reminded him of his favorite blanket when he was little. Paul had given up his blankey a long time ago. But touching the satin edge of this blanket made him remember the good feelings he had had when he touched blankey.

The book was not very long and Mrs. Fenner soon finished it. At the end the little bunny decided not to bother to run away since if he did his mother would always find him no matter what he did.

Paul sighed. "It's a good story. For little kids, I mean. You know."

His mother kissed him good night. "We love you, Paul."

Paul decided maybe he would not bother to take his blanket and pillow underneath the bed. The dark didn't seem so scary anymore and he was getting tired of sleeping under the bed.

Chapter Thirteen

Monday, Paul got a letter from Tiffany. He was very excited. "She wrote me back!" he said. "This letter is from Tiffany!" He looked carefully at the return address—102 Oak Street—before opening the letter. He would like to find it on the map. He would like to see for himself exactly where she had gone.

Dear Paul,
   I have a kitten. He sleeps with me. I have a swing, too. I swing a lot. I do not have to take tennis lessons anymore. I like my new house. My new school is fun, too. I am in the third grade again. I am in the first reading group. If you write me again my name will be Tiffany

Bonner because I am being adopted. My kitten's name is Smokey Bonner. He is adopted, too.

Your friend,
Tiffany

"That's from Tiffany, all right," said Paul. "See that stuff about the first reading group? She always brags about that." Paul was surprised at how good he felt. He started whistling "Yankee Doodle." He had just learned it. "I'm going over to Billy's house," he said.

"Don't stay long, sweetheart. Supper's almost ready."

Paul went to Billy's house and showed Billy how he could whistle "Yankee Doodle."

"Tiffany's got a kitten now," he said.

"You talked to her?"

"She wrote me a letter," said Paul.

"I never get any letters," said Billy. "I get birthday cards, though."

"I've gotten letters before," said Paul. This was the best one, he thought. He was really relieved that Tiffany was okay. It made him feel a whole lot better.

★　　★　　★

When the announcement of Tiffany's adoption was in the paper, Paul's mother showed it to him.

"Tiffany took the middle name of her new mother because she loves her so much," she said. "She's found the right family for her now."

"Can I have another hamburger," said Paul. "I'm still hungry."

Mrs. Fenner smiled. "I think you're having a growth spurt," she said.

That summer Paul went to the YMCA to take intermediate swimming. He saw Tiffany beside the pool. She was with a tall, skinny woman. The woman's hair was turning gray.

Paul yelled. "Hey, Tiffany!" He waved his arms.

He wondered if she remembered who he was. He had grown a lot. He saw her turn to talk to the tall lady. Then they came over.

"Hey, Paul," said Tiffany.

She did remember him. He was glad about that. "Hey, Tiffany. I thought maybe you wouldn't recognize me because I've grown so much."

Paul rose up a little on his tiptoes so he'd

be taller. Tiffany was still a good many inches taller than he was but he was gaining on her.

The woman smiled at Tiffany. She looked like she really liked Tiffany. That made Paul feel good. He wanted to be able to believe that everything was turning out all right, just the way his mother had said.

"You must be the boy who wrote Tiffany the letter," said the lady.

"Yeah. I addressed it and put the stamp on it and everything," said Paul. "And you don't have to tell me you're in the first reading group, Tiffany, because you already told me in the letter."

"Tiffany is such a good reader," said the lady. "But I'll bet you're a good reader, too."

"Not too bad," said Paul modestly.

"My cat Smokey is big now," said Tiffany. "When he purrs he sounds like the motor in the refrigerator."

"I might get a tarantula," said Paul. "The last time I asked my mother, she said, 'We'll see.' I'm working on her. I'm wearing her down."

"Come on in, Paul," Billy yelled.

"I was talking to Tiffany."

"Hey, Tiffany!" yelled Billy and waved from the pool.

"Here I come!" yelled Paul. "Geronimo!" He landed in the water with the biggest splash of all. He was sure Tiffany was impressed.

About the Author

JANICE HARRELL decided she wanted to be a writer when she was in the fourth grade. She grew up in Florida and received her master's and doctorate degrees in eighteenth-century English literature from the University of Florida. After teaching college English for a number of years, she began to write full time.

She lives in Rocky Mount, North Carolina, with her husband, a psychologist, and their daughter. Ms. Harrell is a compulsive traveler—some of the countries she has visited are Greece, France, Egypt, Italy, England, and Spain—and she loves taking photographs.

Read these exciting adventures from Minstrel® Books:

Monica and Dee Ellen have pledged their friendship in ketchup instead of in blood! Together they solve mysteries in *The Ketchup Sisters* by Judith Hollands

•

Ernie learns *How to Survive Third Grade* with the help of a new friend. By Laurie Lawlor

•

All Bertine wanted was a bear. But suddenly she had ten walking, talking Teddies that sprouted from *The Teddy Bear Tree.* By Barbara Dillon

•

Liza's in trouble before class even begins! She thinks *Third Grade is Terrible.* By Barbara Baker

•

James and his friends must find the missing magic lunchbox or they'll have to eat healthy lunches forever! *No Bean Sprouts, Please!* by Constance Hiser

•

Meet Mr. Pin, the penguin detective who can't stay out of trouble: *The Mysterious Cases of Mr. Pin* and *Mr. Pin: The Chocolate Files,* by Mary Elise Monsell

These titles and many more fun books are available from

 MINSTREL® BOOKS

Published by Pocket Books